# David Walliams

## PRESENTS...

*For Ruby and her beautiful smile.*

With love,

Uncle David x

*To Wendy,*

*who suffers with a smile.*

T.R.

# GERON

First published in hardback by HarperCollins *Children's Books* in 2018

First published in this edition in 2021

HarperCollins *Children's Books* is a division of HarperCollins *Publishers* Ltd.

1 London Bridge Street, London SE1 9GF

www.harpercollins.co.uk

HarperCollins*Publishers*

1st Floor, Watermarque Building, Ringsend Road, Dublin 4, Ireland

Text copyright © David Walliams 2018. Illustrations copyright © Tony Ross 2018

Cover lettering of author's name copyright © Quentin Blake 2010

David Walliams and Tony Ross assert the moral right to be identified as the author and illustrator of the work respectively.

A CIP catalogue record for this title is available from the British Library.

3 5 7 9 10 8 6 4

Printed in Great Britain by Bell and Bain Ltd, Glasgow

978–0–00–827979–0

# IMO

Illustrated by the artistic genius

## Tony Ross

HarperCollins *Children's Books*

At the bottomest bottom of the world lived a huge colony of emperor penguins. All the eggs were being kept warm by their dads when one baby penguin **hatched.**

His name was

# GERONIMO.

"Let's fly!" he announced, flapping his wings as fast as he could.

"Penguins **can't fly**, son!" replied his father.

"Of course they can, Dad! Otherwise what have we got **wings** for?

Watch!"

With his feet as skis, the baby penguin used a snowy slope as a runway.

"**GERONIMO!**"

he cried as he sped
faster
and
faster.

He hit a bump on the slope and...

took off.

Whizz!

For a few glorious seconds Geronimo

sailed through the air.

"Dad! Look! I can fly!"

The baby frantically flapped his wings before dropping through the air like a stone. He landed in the freezing-cold sea with a plop!

"You see, son, penguins **can't** fly," said Dad.

Geronimo looked sad.

"But it's all I **dream** about, Dad. There **must** be a way for my dream to come true."

Geronimo spied an elephant seal dozing on the ice. He leaped on to the seal's big **wobbly tummy** to use it as a trampoline and launched himself into the air.

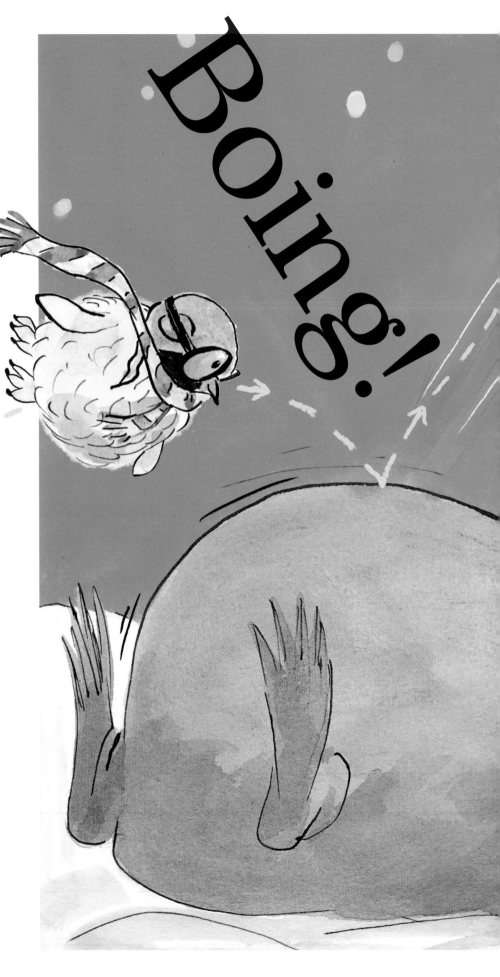

Boing!

Next Geronimo paddled out to sea and clambered on top of a big blue whale, sitting right on top of its **blowhole.**

# Splurt!

Air shot up Geronimo's bottom and **blasted** him into the sky like a rocket.

**"Dad!** Look! I can **fly!"**

As soon as the whale stopped blowing, Geronimo plummeted. The angry whale flicked its tail…

Swish!

…batting the little penguin across the sky.

"Dad! Look! I can—"

but before he could say "FLY" he slammed straight into an iceberg.

Doof!

His dad had to give him **beak-to-beak** resuscitation.

"It's time to **give up** on your dream, son!"

"**Never,** Dad! Dreams **can** come true.

I know it."

Every night when Dad tucked Geronimo under his ice sheet the baby penguin would **dream** the same **dream**

of **flight,** of soaring

high in the air, swooping and twirling.

Touching the clouds.
The king of the sky.

His dad had had that dream too when he was young...

The next morning, Geronimo leaped on the back of an unsuspecting **albatross**.

"Look! Dad! I can **fly!**"

But not for long…

The overloaded albatross crashed headfirst into a pod of baby seals, knocking them into the sea like bowling pins.

The Emperor emperor penguin turned to Dad.

"You have to tell your son,
once and for all,

penguins **can't**
**fly!**"

With a heavy heart, Dad told his son,

"No more trying to **fly**, Geronimo.

The **DREAM** is **over**."

Dad felt awful as a single **tear**

rolled down his son's face.

So awful that later that night, while Geronimo was sleeping, he called a meeting of the whole colony.

"Fellow penguins, are we sure it is absolutely impossible for us to fly?"

"Yes! Of course!"

barked the Emperor emperor penguin.

"There must be a way!" replied Dad.

"No!"
"Never!"
"Fool!"

"Didn't YOU ever dream of flying?" asked Dad.

This silenced the colony. They'd **all** had that dream when they were young.

"Let's put our bird brains together, and see!" said Dad.

That's exactly what they did. By the time the sun came up, the colony had a plan...

When Geronimo woke that morning, the **strangest** sight greeted him. The entire colony of penguins was
# upside down.

"What's
**happened?"**
asked
Geronimo.

"What do you mean, **what's happened?**" replied Dad,
who, like all the others, was standing on his head.

"You are all **upside down!**"

"NO! *You're* upside down!

Come jump off the ice, and you will soar into the sky!" Dad pointed at the sea.

"Yes!" replied the whole colony.

"Yes, that's the sky," said the Emperor emperor penguin,

pointing at the sea.

"Now come on, Geronimo," said Dad.
"Show us that dreams **can** come true.
That penguins **really can fly!**"

So with that Geronimo

made a giant leap...

splash!

The little penguin flapped his wings and **zoomed** through the water, thinking it was the **sky**.

"I can **fly!**"

"I can fly!"

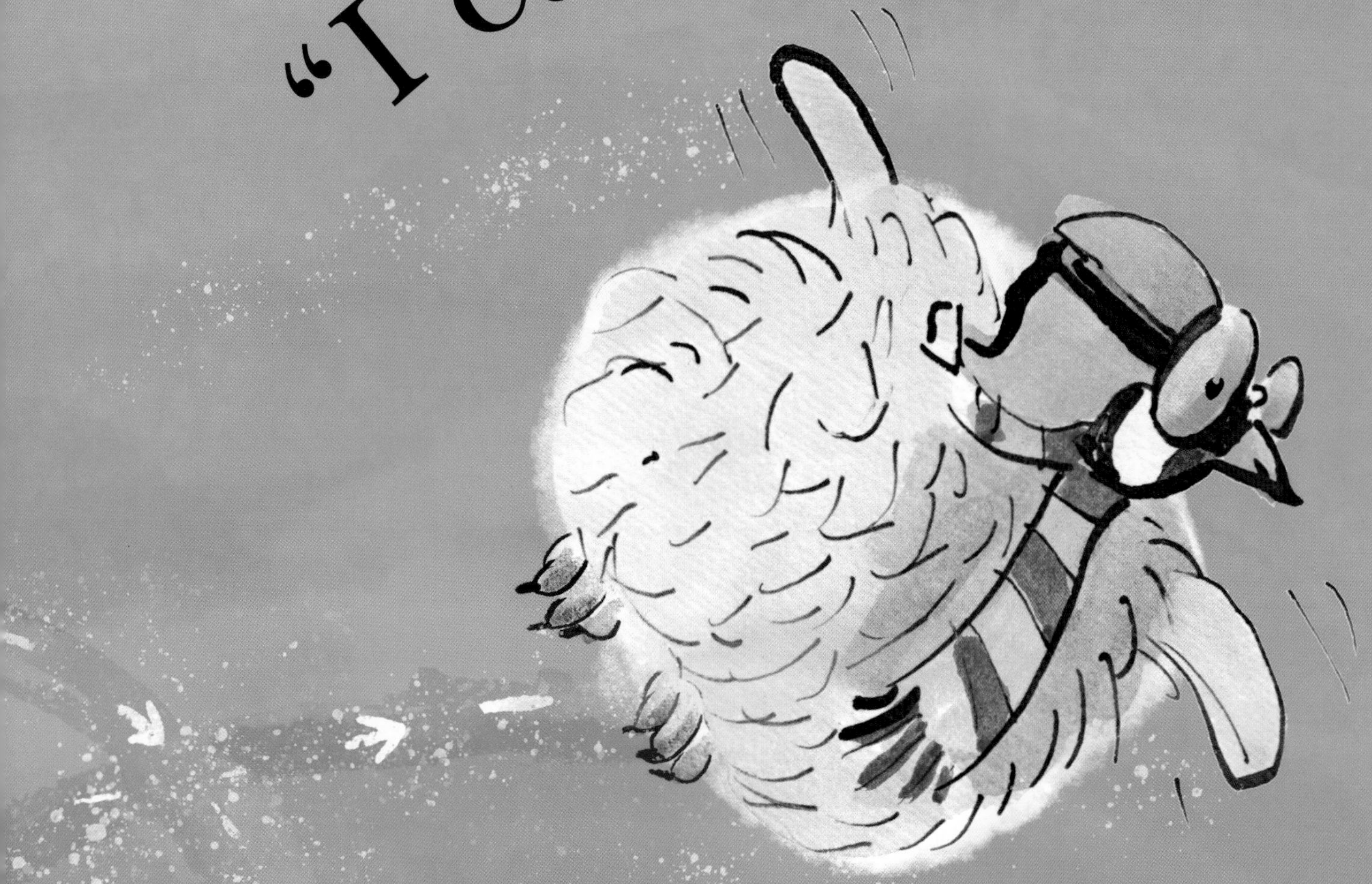

"I can fly!" he yelled.

On Dad's signal, the colony
dived in too.

Splish!
Splash!
Splosh!

Dad held his son's wing. The pair shared a smile.

Together they looped the loop, very nearly bumping into an iceberg.

"Be careful of the clouds!"

called out Dad.

They passed a **killer whale.**

"Dad? Why is that whale floating upside down in the sky?" asked Geronimo.

"He must have jumped," said Dad.

"Oh!"

Dad watched with pride as his son soared up, up, up.

"Dad!
Look!
I can fly!"

"I'm king of the sky!"

Sometimes, with a little help and some upside down penguins, dreams really can come true.